J

A NOTE TO PARENTS

When your children are ready to "step into reading," giving them the right books—and lots of them—is as crucial as giving them the right food to eat. **Step into Reading Books** present exciting stories and information reinforced with lively, colorful illustrations that make learning to read fun, satisfying, and worthwhile. They are priced so that acquiring an entire library of them is affordable. And they are beginning readers with an important difference—they're written on four levels.

Step 1 Books, with their very large type and extremely simple vocabulary, have been created for the very youngest readers. **Step 2 Books** are both longer and slightly more difficult. **Step 3 Books,** written to mid-second-grade reading levels, are for the child who has acquired even greater reading skills. **Step 4 Books** offer exciting nonfiction for the increasingly proficient reader.

Children develop at different ages. **Step into Reading Books,** with their four levels of reading, are designed to help children become good—and interested—readers *faster*. The grade levels assigned to the four steps—preschool through grade 1 for Step 1, grades 1 through 3 for Step 2, grades 2 and 3 for Step 3, and grades 2 through 4 for Step 4—are intended only as guides. Some children move through all four steps very rapidly; others climb the steps over a period of several years. These books will help your child "step into reading" in style!

Library of Congress Cataloging-in-Publication Data:
O'Connor, Jane. The teeny tiny woman. (Step into reading. A Step 1 book). SUMMARY: A teeny tiny woman who puts a teeny tiny bone she finds in a churchyard away in a cupboard before she goes to sleep is awakened by a voice demanding the return of the bone.
  [1. Ghosts—Folklore. 2. Folklore—England] I. Alley, R. W. (Robert W.), ill. II. Title. III. Series: Step into reading. A Step 1 book. PZ8.1.O24Te 1986   398.2′5′0942   [E]   86-485
ISBN: 0-394-88320-9 (trade); 0-394-98320-3 (lib. bdg.)

Manufactured in the United States of America

35 36 37 38 39 40

STEP INTO READING is a trademark of Random House, Inc.

Step into Reading

The
Teeny Tiny
Woman

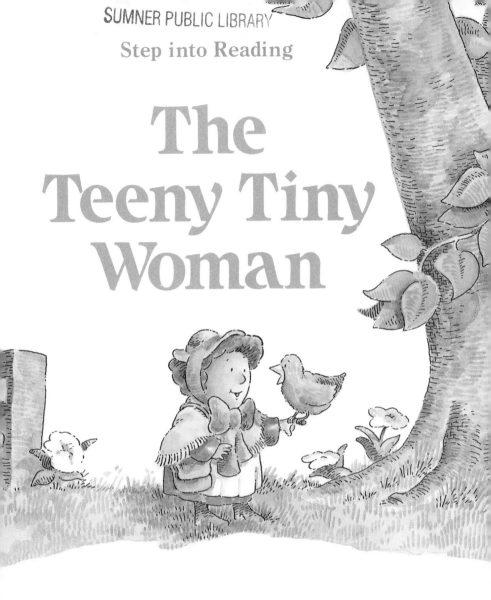

retold by Jane O'Connor
illustrated by R.W. Alley

A Step 1 Book

Random House 🏠 New York

A teeny tiny woman
lived in a teeny tiny house.

One day she put on
her teeny tiny hat.

She got her teeny tiny bag.

And she went for
a teeny tiny walk.

Soon the teeny tiny woman
came to a teeny tiny gate.

She opened
the teeny tiny gate
and went into
a teeny tiny yard.

9

There she saw
a teeny tiny bone
on a teeny tiny grave.
"I can make some
teeny tiny soup
with this teeny tiny bone,"
said the teeny tiny woman.

The teeny tiny woman
put the teeny tiny bone
in her teeny tiny bag.

She went through
the teeny tiny gate.

She walked
and walked
and walked
all the way back
to her teeny tiny house.

The teeny tiny woman
opened her teeny tiny door.

"My teeny tiny feet are tired,"
said the teeny tiny woman.

"I will not make
my teeny tiny soup now."

The teeny tiny woman
put the teeny tiny bone
in a teeny tiny cupboard.

Then she got into
her teeny tiny bed
for a teeny tiny nap.

Soon a teeny tiny

voice called:

"Give me my bone!"

The teeny tiny woman
was a teeny tiny bit scared.

"I must have had
a teeny tiny dream,"
she said.

The teeny tiny woman
had a teeny tiny glass
of milk.

Then she got back into
her teeny tiny bed.

Soon she fell asleep.

It was not long before
the teeny tiny voice
called out again.
"Give me my bone!"

The teeny tiny woman
woke up.

She was so scared
she hid under
her teeny tiny covers.

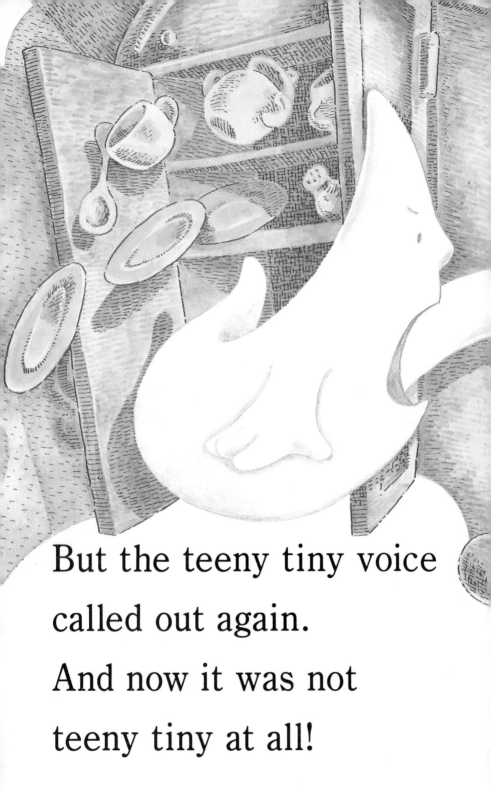

But the teeny tiny voice
called out again.
And now it was not
teeny tiny at all!

The teeny tiny woman
peeked out from
her teeny tiny covers.

She said,

"TAKE IT!"

And that is the end of
this teeny tiny story.